MOUNTAIN BOY

Story by
ANNA CATHERINE JOSEPHS

Illustrations by
BILL ERSLAND

A Carnival Press Book   Raintree Publishers Inc.

In memory of my grandfather, Howard A. Zachary,
youngest son of Thomas (Tommy) Robard Zachary,
who, along with my grandmother, taught me to
know and love the Blue Ridge Mountains.

— A.C.J.

For Christopher and Nathaniel, stay inquisitive
and maintain those adventurous spirits!

— B.E.

Published by Raintree Publishers Inc.
330 East Kilbourn Avenue, Milwaukee, Wisconsin 53202.

Book Design: Su Lund

Printed in the United States of America   2 3 4 5 6 7 8 9 0 89 88 87 86 85

Library of Congress Cataloging in Publication Data
Josephs, Anna Catherine.   Mountain boy.   "A Carnival Press book."
Summary: Describes how fourteen-year-old Thomas Zachary helped a group of escaped Union prisoners
elude the Confederate soldiers in the mountains of North Carolina and make it to freedom.   1. United
States—History—Civil War, 1861-1865—Prisons and prisoners—Juvenile literature.   2. North Carolina—
History—Civil War, 1861-1865—Prisons and prisoners—Juvenile literature.   3. Zachary, Thomas—
Juvenile literature.   4. North Carolina—Biography—Juvenile literature. [1. United States—History—
Civil War, 1861-1865—Prisons and prisoners. 2. Escapes. 3. Zachary, Thomas] I. Ersland, William, ill.
II. Title.   E611.J66 1985   973.7'71   85-12238   ISBN 0-940742-51-9

Tommy Zachary was only fourteen years old, but already he was a real mountain man. His father had long been sick, so Tommy — my great-grandfather — quit school in the fifth grade at age ten to become the man of the family. He knew how to cook, chop wood, track wild animals, and, most important, how to find his way through the dense mountain woods with only the sun and the stars as his compass. But he dreamed of going back to school someday.

Tommy lived with his bedridden father, his mother, and his baby sister in a small log cabin in the mountains of North Carolina. His other five sisters were married, and his seven brothers were off fighting in the Civil War, some on the Southern side and some on the Northern side.

It was during the coldest part of the winter that a small band of Union soldiers came upon the Zachary cabin well-hidden in the woods in Cashiers Valley. When the soldiers knocked, it was young Tommy who opened the door. They looked ragged and dirty, but Tommy was not afraid. He and his parents listened as the soldiers told about their escape from a Confederate prison in Columbia, South Carolina, on the night of November 10, 1864.

9

The prison was so crowded and infested with rats that the soldiers were willing to risk capture and death rather than stay in such an awful place. After many hours of secret work, they were able to escape through a tunnel dug with their hands. Their goal was to get to the Union lines in Knoxville, Tennessee, by crossing the Blue Ridge Mountains.

The men traveled only at night and never by public roads. All they had to eat were sweet potatoes, which they got in the fields, or cornbread and sorghum syrup that they got from the black people along the way. These people were always their friends and helped them because they knew the escaping men were fighting for their freedom, too.

Sometimes the men were chased by Confederate soldiers, but they always managed to escape. Once, the Union soldiers raided a Rebel wagon train loaded with hams, bacon, honey, chestnuts, clothes, and blankets. They shared these with the people who were willing to give them a place to hide during the day.

15

It was slow traveling because the enemy was everywhere. The men were very discouraged, but they were relieved when they finally reached the mountains of North Carolina. They knew the mountaineers were often Union sympathizers and could be counted on to help them out. Tommy Zachary's father was well-known as a supporter of the Union cause.

The soldiers needed a guide who knew the mountains, who could lead them on the back trails and around the treacherous laurel shrub "hells." When they told Tommy what they wanted, Tommy begged his father to let him go. The boy was needed at home, but his father wanted to help the Union men. He knew Tommy was a brave and capable boy, so he finally agreed to let Tommy be their guide. His mother packed some warm clothes and food and kissed him goodbye.

It was a journey that Tommy would never forget. When he and the small band of men set out, the trees were covered with ice, the ground was slippery, and there was about two feet of snow on the ground. Along the way, they had to hide in caves for days and days, hoping the Southerners' bloodhounds wouldn't find them. They were almost freezing, but they could not have campfires because the enemy would see the smoke and the firelight and know where to find them.

When Tommy and the men could not find caves, they had to build huts out of chestnut bark chinked with moss. The wind that blew through the cracks in the huts made an eerie sound. Their food was running out, but they couldn't shoot a gun to kill squirrels or rabbits because the enemy would hear the gunshots.

The soldiers longed to reach Tennessee, but they were so cold and tired and hungry that only the memory of their horrible days in prison kept them from turning back in search of food and warmth. Tommy was terribly homesick, but he knew if he left the men now, the soldiers would be completely lost and would never see their homes again. He had to keep his promise. Another thing kept him from turning back. The men had promised to pay his way to college if they ever reached the Union lines.

It took Tommy and the soldiers fifty-two days to reach Sweetwater, Tennessee, about one hundred and twenty miles from Cashiers Valley and Tommy's home. The band of ragged soldiers said goodbye to Tommy, and he left at once for home. He made the trip back with no trouble because the Confederate soldiers hadn't found out about his secret journey. When he got home, his mother and father were very happy to see him.

Tommy got letters from Captain Bassett, the leader of the prisoners, for many years. When Bassett died, his wife continued to write to the boy who had brought her husband back during the war. But no money ever came. Even though he never got the education he had dreamed about, Tommy wasn't mad. But he often thought of the things he would have learned in college.

My great-grandfather Tommy remained an adventurous man, homesteading in Kansas with his own family and later riding over the Blue Ridge Mountains, planting trees like Johnny Appleseed. Many of his trees still grow all over North Carolina, especially around the old home place in the mountains where the Zachary family still takes care of them and where I love to visit.

Every summer nine-year-old Anna Catherine Josephs visits her grandmother, Alberta Zachary, in Cashiers, North Carolina. The eleven-acre mountain homestead has been in the family for generations. It is where Anna's great-grandfather, Thomas Robard Zachary, grew up, and where this story takes place. The story is one that Anna has heard her grandparents tell many times.

Anna's love for her heritage is obvious when she describes the beauty of the mountains: "In the summer in the Blue Ridge Mountains there are flowers and beautiful green grass. The trees have pretty green leaves, and everyone goes swimming and has a good time."

When she's not spending the summers in North Carolina, Anna lives with her family in Pensacola, Florida. Her father, Allen, her mother, Julie, an older sister, Laura, and a younger sister, Maricarmen, are all very proud of her. Although there have been other published writers in the family, Anna is the youngest to be so honored.

All of Anna's fourth grade classmates at the Creative Learning Center in Pensacola entered Raintree's 1985 *Publish-A-Book Contest* to fulfill a class assignment. When Eileen Dunkerley, Anna's teacher and sponsor in the contest, asked each student to write a Heritage story, Anna's grandmother encouraged her to tell her great-grandfather's story. As winner of the nationwide contest, Anna was awarded a cash prize by Raintree Publishers, in addition to having her book, *Mountain Boy*, published.

The twenty second-prize winners of the Raintree *Publish-A-Book Contest* were: Karen Elizabeth Bowen, Placitas, New Mexico; Neil Erickson, Cloquet, Minnesota; Jacob Flint, Baytown, Texas; David Frost, Portland, Oregon; Troy Fujimura, Culver, Indiana; Harmony Goodman, Malibu, California; Deana Rae Harrison, St. John, Kansas; Clint Holm, Walker, Louisiana; Laura Honey, Manassas, Virginia; Greg Johnson, Memphis, Tennessee; Teddy Krey, Windsor, Ontario; Jerilynn Long, Crownpoint, New Mexico; Huong Mai, Aurora, Illinois; Vivek Maru, Brookfield, Connecticut; Kristine Miller, New Milford, New Jersey; Jacob Matthew Humel Montwieler, Washington, D.C.; Tony Rodriguez, Wendell, Idaho; Sara Spanel, Wahpeton, North Dakota; Luke Weinstock, Westport, Connecticut; and Stuart D. Wright, Chicago, Illinois.

Artist Bill Ersland was born in Des Moines, Iowa. After graduating from Iowa State University with a major in art, he worked for a large Midwestern art studio for ten years. Bill now lives and works in Stillwater, Minnesota, dividing his time between family and art.